Postman Pat
and the
Harvest Parcel

Story by **John Cunliffe** Pictures by **Joan Hickson**
From the original Television designs by **Ivor Wood**

Scholastic Children's Books
Commonwealth House, 1-19 New Oxford Street
London WC1A 1NU

A division of Scholastic Publications Ltd
London ~ New York ~ Toronto ~ Sydney ~ Auckland

First published in the UK by Scholastic Publications Ltd, 1989
This edition published in1993
Text copyright © John Cunliffe 1989 and 1993
Illustrations copyright © Scholastic Publications Ltd
and Woodland Animations Ltd 1989

A longer version of this story has been previously published as a Handy Hippo

ISBN 0 590 54138 2

10 9 8 7 6 5 4 3

Typeset by Rapid Reprographics Ltd
Printed in Italy by L.E.G.O. S.p.A.

It had been a good summer in Greendale.
Pat met Peter Fogg on his way home.

"You'll be wanting to get that barley in,
while this good weather lasts," said Pat.

"I'm going for the combine first thing
on Monday," said Peter.

"Thanks for telling me," said Pat. "I'll
be on the look out for you."

The combine harvester is so big that nothing can get past it on the narrow Greendale roads. Cars have to get into a layby or a gateway, to let it go past.

When Katy and Tom heard the combine was coming, they were very excited. Sometimes, Peter would give them a ride on it, so high up that it was almost like flying. And later they could play lovely games with the bales of straw; jumping, and hiding, and making straw houses.

Pat met Peter with the combine. He got his van into a gateway, just in time.

"Morning Peter!" shouted Pat. Then he followed Peter along to Greendale Farm.

When Peter had the combine safely
parked, Katy and Tom danced round him,
both talking at once, "Can we have a
ride...can we come and watch...can we have
a picnic...can we drive...can we...can
we...?"

7

"Now you two leave Peter alone till he gets his wits back," said Mrs Pottage, "and, if you're very good, and very careful, and do just as you're told, we'll all go to the field and see the combine and have a picnic."

"And I'll come when I've delivered all my letters," said Pat, "and give a hand with loading the bales. I'll bring my sandwiches, too, and I might save you a chocolate biscuit."

"Ooooh! Goody!" shouted Katy and Tom.

"But Peter's going first, without us," said Mrs Pottage, "and we're not going until he's done at least half the field, and there's a good safe part to play in. They're dangerous things, these harvesters, and we don't want any accidents."

"Please," said Katy. "Can I wear my new jumper?"

"You can," said Mrs Pottage, "if you promise not to lose it."

Katy and Tom ran to get their jumpers
to show Pat.

"Lovely," said Pat, "but I'd best be on
my way. See you later! Cheerio!"

Pat was on his way. As he called on the people of Greendale with their letters, he told them about the arrival of the combine at Greendale Farm. He had some letters for the Reverend Timms.

"I'll pop round with my camera," said the Reverend, "when I've finished my sermon. Now do make sure they keep some sheaves for Harvest Festival."

Pat called at Thompson Ground.

"We're too busy with our haymaking to come just now," said Dorothy, "but take them a tin of cakes, with my love."

Pat called on Granny Dryden. She was busy parcelling up a new jumper, to send to little Yasmin, in London.

"Oh, Pat," said Granny Dryden. "I've gone and used up all my string, and I wanted to give you this parcel to put in the post today. Now what shall I do?"

"Don't worry," said Pat. "I'm sure to have some string. Let's see, now...Yes, here we are. Just the job..."

Pat helped Granny Dryden to tie her parcel up with some good post office knots.

13

Then he told her about Peter bringing the combine, and everyone going off to join in and give a hand with the harvest.

"Oh, I love harvest time," she said. "Ever since I was a girl, I've never missed it. I'll have a stroll down this afternoon. I'm going to put some scones in the oven, and they're just the thing for a picnic."

"Lovely," said Pat. "Bye!"

Pat called on George Lancaster, at Intake Farm.

"Hardboiled eggs," said George. "I'll bring plenty for everyone."

Pat called on Ted Glen.

"I know," said Ted. "I'll be down with the baler, later on. I hope they keep those children out of harm's way, till I've done."

Pat called on Miss Hubbard.

"They'll need plenty to drink," she said. "It's jolly thirsty work, harvesting. I'll bring some cider and lemonade, and a flask of tea."

Pat went on his way. He went all along the valley with his letters and parcels.

When Pat had finished all his work for the day, he said, "Come on, Jess. Time for a bite to eat. And let's see how they're getting on with that combine."

It was like a party, in that harvest-field.
Mrs Pottage was handing round sandwiches,
Granny Dryden was going round with a
basket of scones, and Miss Hubbard was
pouring drinks. Katy and Tom and most of
the children from the village were running
and playing in the stubble.

The Reverend Timms was taking
pictures of everyone. Peter had almost
finished cutting the corn. He had stopped to
join in the picnic, and the combine stood
quietly at the far side of the field. There was
a trailer full of barley, and long lines of straw
lying across the field.

Just as Pat sat down with a glass of cider, there was the sound of a tractor in the lane.

"Look out, everyone!" called Mrs Pottage. "It's Ted with the baler! All to the sides of the field, please!"

The baler came rattling into the field behind Ted, and they all scurried to the hedges.

"We don't want anyone getting baled up in a parcel of hay!" said the Reverend Timms.

The binder rumbled round the field, gathering up the straw that the combine had left. It made the straw into neat parcels, and tied them up with string, just like Granny Dryden's parcel.

When the binder had gone off to the far side of the big field, Katy said, "Please, mum, can we play with the bales, now?" "Well...if you keep over this side, and well away from the baler," said Mrs Pottage. "Promise?"

"Promise, promise, promise," said all the children, and off they went, running and jumping amongst the bales.

What lovely things they were to play with! You could hide behind them for hide and seek. You could jump from the top of them.

If you asked Pat to help you lift them, you could build straw houses with them. You could build bridges, and staircases, and castles with them. You could slide down them, sit on them, creep under them, lie on them. The children had a wonderful time.

It was getting late in the afternoon, and the trees were stretching their shadows far out across the great field. More than once, Mrs Pottage had called out, "Come on, children, time to go home." And more than once the children had shouted, "Just a bit longer."

Miss Hubbard packed up and rode off on her bicycle, with her cider bottles clinking down the lane. Granny Dryden was off home to put the kettle on. And still the children played.

The mothers came from the village to call their children home, and Katy and Tom were left at last alone, with Pat and Jess snoozing in the sun by the hedge, and Mrs Pottage saying, "Now it really is time to go," and walking about picking up sandals, and cups, and all the things that people had dropped and forgotten. Then she said, "Where *is* Katy's new woolly?"

"And where is my hat?" said Pat, sitting up and rubbing his eyes. "Bless me, is it that time? We'll be missing our tea. Come on, Jess, help us to sniff out a hat and a woolly jumper."

They searched all among the bales of straw. It was like looking in a maze. But there was no sign of Pat's hat or Katy's jumper.

Katy looked as though she might begin to cry quite soon.

"I have a feeling it'll turn up," said Pat. "Hi! What's that?"

Pat was staring at a bale of straw as he was speaking. Between the ends of the straw, he could see something blue. He poked his fingers into the straw, and pulled at the tightly-packed straw parcel.

"What have you found, Pat?" said Tom.

"Well, I'm not sure...but I'll tell you when I get this parcel open. There's no address on it, so it's all right to open it."

Pat cut the string round the bale. He pushed his hand into the straw, and pulled out a sleeve...a woollen sleeve.

27

"Well... just look at this!" said Pat.

"Is it...?" said Mrs Pottage.

"Katy's jumper?" said Pat. "I think so. Easy does it. We mustn't pull too hard. My goodness, this is a good parcel. Dry your eyes, Katy. Look, it is your jumper. You must have dropped it and then it got baled up with the straw."

It took a long time to get the jumper out of the bale, and it needed a good shaking, but it was all right.

"Just look at that bale," said Mrs Pottage. "Dad will wonder what happened to it when he sees it."

"What about Pat's hat?" said Katy.

"It might be in another bale," said Tom. They looked at all the bales, but there was no sign of Pat's hat.

"Don't be sad, Pat," said Katy. "I'll find it."

"It's all right," said Pat. "I can wear my old one. But wherever can it be?"

They looked a little longer, in the hedge, and in the long grass at the edge of the field, but they didn't find it. So they all went home to tea.

It was Katy who found Pat's hat in the
end, but he had a long time to wait for it. It
was in the winter, when the cornfield was
covered in snow. Katy was helping Peter to
put fresh straw out for the cows.

Deep in the middle of another bale, there was Pat's hat, as good as new! Katy shouted just in time to stop Peter from putting his hay-fork through the middle of it. She took it into the house, and asked mum for a brush, and gave it a good cleaning.